KV-578-929

In the **Beginner Reader** level, **Step 12** builds on the phonics learning covered in previous steps and focuses on different pronunciations of familiar letter combinations.

Special features:

Phonically decodable text builds reading confidence

Short sentences with simple language

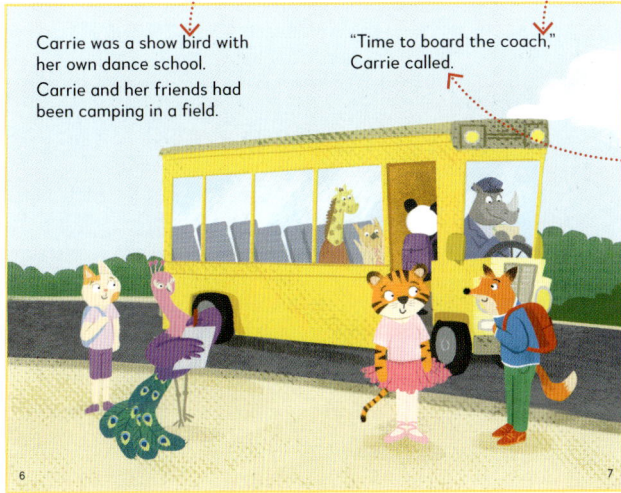

Carrie was a show bird with her own dance school.
Carrie and her friends had been camping in a field.

"Time to board the coach," Carrie called.

6   7

Repetition of sounds in different words

Practice of words that cannot be sounded out

Summary page to reinforce learning

Story words

Can you match these words to the pictures?

gold boots

shoes

tiger

city

bow

ladybird

Tricky words

These tricky words are in the story you have just read. They cannot be sounded out. Can you memorize them and read them super fast?

when	said
could	on
so	called

16   17

Ladybird

Educational Consultants: Geraldine Taylor and James Clements
Phonics and Book Banding Consultant: Kate Ruttle

LADYBIRD BOOKS

UK | USA | Canada | Ireland | Australia
India | New Zealand | South Africa

Ladybird Books is part of the Penguin Random House group of companies
whose addresses can be found at global.penguinrandomhouse.com.

www.penguin.co.uk   www.puffin.co.uk   www.ladybird.co.uk

Penguin
Random House
UK

First published 2020
This edition published 2024
001

Written by Katie Woolley
Text copyright © Ladybird Books Ltd, 2020, 2024
Illustrations by Amy Zhing
Illustrations copyright © Ladybird Books Ltd, 2020, 2024

The moral right of the author and illustrator has been asserted

Printed in China

The authorized representative in the EEA is Penguin Random House Ireland,
Morrison Chambers, 32 Nassau Street, Dublin D02 YH68

A CIP catalogue record for this book is available from the British Library

ISBN: 978-0-241-56441-7

All correspondence to:
Ladybird Books
Penguin Random House Children's
One Embassy Gardens, 8 Viaduct Gardens, London SW11 7BW

CARRIE'S DANCE SCHOOL

Written by Katie Woolley
Illustrated by Amy Zhing

Carrie was a show bird with her own dance school.

Carrie and her friends had been camping in a field.

"Time to board the coach,"
Carrie called.

7

The coach set off down the road. "I can see snow!" said Bob the owl. "It will be cold when we get back to the city."

Izzy the tiger was the star
of the dance school show.
She could leap and twirl
high in the sky.

One day Izzy was feeling
very cross.

"My feet hurt," she shouted.
"I need new shoes!"

So Izzy took the train into the
giant city.

She put on lots of shoes but she did not like any of them.

"Look at the silly yellow bows," she moaned. "I can't see my toes!"

The ladybird in the shop heard
Izzy shout. She found her
a special pair of shoes.

"These would be perfect."
Izzy smiled. "Thank you!"

That night, the dance school show was a big success.

The crowd went wild for Izzy
and her gold snow boots!

Story words

Can you match these words
to the pictures?

gold

boots

shoes

tiger

city

bow

ladybird

Tricky words

These tricky words are in the story you have just read. They cannot be sounded out. Can you memorize them and read them super fast?

when   said

could   on

so   called

CARRIE'S COLD

Written by Katie Woolley
Illustrated by Amy Zhing

Carrie the show bird was
feeling very ill.

"I have got a cold. I need to be
in bed."

Carrie's friends said they would help her get better.

Carrie was hot and cold.
She called Izzy the tiger.

"Could you find me a hat?"
she asked.

Carrie was hungry. She called George the giant panda.

"Could you bring me bread and soup to eat?" she said.

Carrie was feeling chirpy now.
She called Chris the cat.

"Could you fetch me a chocolate ice cream?" she asked.

The next day Carrie was better.
She tried to find her friends.

They were all sick and tucked up in bed.

"We have all got your cold!" they cried.

Now it was Carrie's turn to help her friends get better!

Story words

Can you match these words
to the pictures?

ice
cream

hat

giant
panda

bread

soup

bed